This book is dedicated to my wonderful friend
Norma Luckemeyer.

Norma illustrated the first three Clinker books
CLINKER'S FLEA
CLINKER'S SHADOW
CLINKER MEETS THE FLYING SQUIRREL
& also JOHNNY COALBOY
(and I couldn't have done it without her).

1

CLINKER'S CHRISTMAS STAR

By

Kay Witschen

Illustrated by
Tessa Kay Witschen-Boelz

CLINKER'S CHRISTMAS STAR

Clinker and his new friend Lacy had fun playing tag in the woods.

"Lacy, I'm tired. Let's sit down for a few minutes then head for home."

"Good idea, Clinker. I'm worn out too."

"Wow, did you see that falling star?" asked Clinker.

"No, I was looking the wrong way," replied Lacy. "But I bet I can spot the 'Big Dipper' faster than you can!"

"Just wait until we get out of the woods and we will see who can spot the 'Big Dipper' first," said Clinker as they started on their way home.

At the very same moment they both spotted the 'Big Dipper' but that was not all they saw.

"Look," said Clinker, "another star is falling."

"Don't you wonder what happens to a star when it falls?"

"I guess we will probably never know the answer to that, Lacy."

As the dogs continued on their way home, all of a sudden they heard the strangest sound.

"What was that?" Clinker said as his ears perked up.

"I don't know, Clinker, it sounds like crying."

The dogs kept very quiet and soon they heard it again. "Boo Hoo, Boo Hoo."

"Come on Lacy, let's see where that noise is coming from."

"Shh, Lacy, look over here. What is it?"

"I don't know, but it sure is crying, WHATEVER it is."

> *"I'm a star*
> *Can't you see*
> *I want to go home*
> *Can you please help me?"*

"We didn't mean to insult you. How did you get here?" asked Clinker.

9

"I was visiting Sue
But fell from the sky
I couldn't stop
And don't know why."

By now the dogs realized there was nothing for them to be afraid of.

"We don't know what to do to help you," Clinker said. "If you tell us what

to do maybe we can figure out something. Do you have a name?"

"Of course I do
I'm very new
Momma named me
Her Baby Blue."

"Well, Baby Blue," said Lucy, "how do the other new stars get around

without falling to earth?"

"Momma told me
What to do
Now I'll tell
The words to you."

"Count one, two
To visit Sue
Then go to three
And home to me."

"And that's what you said?" asked Clinker.

In between sobs, Baby Blue told the dogs that she said it but nothing

happened.

"Calm down, then try it again," said Lacy. "Maybe it will work this time."

Baby Blue said the words again:

"Count one, two
To visit Sue
Then go to three
And home to me."

Nothing happened! Baby Blue was crying so hard by now that she could

hardly talk.

"I'm so afraid Momma
I'll never roam
If you please, please
Bring me back home."

"Clinker, what are we going to do with her?" said Lacy.

"Just wait, I'll think of something," said Clinker. "Baby Blue, can you walk?"

The little star started to move but it was more like a little hop. By this time snowflakes were starting to fall.

"Oh my, Oh my
What's touching me
It feels so strange
And I can't see."

"It's only snow and it won't hurt you," said Clinker. "We'll take you to a cave where you'll be safe from the snow. And please don't be sad. There has to be some way for you to get back home."

"Lacy, why don't you go back home and change our Christmas Eve plans. See if the animals will come out to a spot near here and we can stay close to Baby Blue."

Clinker stayed in the cave and watched over the little star.

"Can you twinkle, Baby Blue?" asked Clinker.

Baby Blue giggled!

"Of course I can
But why should I
What I need to do
Is learn to fly."

"I have this little favor to ask," said Clinker. "All of our animal friends will gather here in the woods tonight because it's Christmas Eve. We don't have a star for our Christmas tree. Would you help us out?"

"You've been so kind
I guess I can
Help you with
Your Christmas plan."

Soon the animals were gathered around the tree.

"We have a new friend to introduce to you," said Clinker. "This is Baby Blue, a star that fell from the sky."

"OH, MY GOODNESS"

"SURELY A MIRACLE"

"WOW"

"AWESOME"

"I DON'T BELIEVE IT"

"SCARY"

"COOL"

"FAR OUT"

"It's scary for Baby Blue, for she doesn't know how to get back to her Momma. But for tonight, she'll be our tree topper, if we can help her get up there."

Soon Baby Blue was sitting at the top of the Christmas tree. When she began to twinkle the forest lit up for as far as the animals could see.

"Oh," said Lacy. "Have you ever seen anything so beautiful?"

"Never," said Clinker. All of the animals agreed.

Suddenly a loud voice called out:

> *"Is that you*
> *My Baby Blue*
> *I've looked everywhere*
> *For you."*

The glow from Momma Star lit up the entire sky.

"Momma please
Come get me
I'm lighting up
This Christmas tree."

"Baby Blue, say these words and you will be home!"

"One, two, three
And home to me."

Baby Blue said goodbye to all the animals and wished them a Merry

Christmas.

"Clinker and Lacy
I love you
Always remember
Your Baby Blue."

Then Baby Blue said the words that her Momma told her and in a second she was back home.

The animals agreed that this was a Christmas Eve they would NEVER EVER forget.

THE END